HELLO READING!

D0449153

"HELLO READING™ books are a perfect introduction to reading. Brief sentences full of word repetition and full-color pictures stress visual clues to help a child take the first important steps toward reading. Mastering HELLO READING™ books will build children's reading confidence and give them the enthusiasm to stand on their own in the world of words."

—Bee Cullinan
Past President of the International Reading
Association, Professor in New York University's
Early Childhood and Elementary Education Program

"Readers aren't born, they're made. Desire is planted—planted by parents who work at it."

—Jim Trelease
author of *The Read Aloud Handbook*

"When I was a classroom reading teacher, I recognized the importance of good stories in making children understand that reading is more than just recognizing words. I saw that children who get excited about reading and who have ready access to books make noticeably greater gains in reading comprehension and fluency. The development of the HELLO READING™ series grows out of this experience."

—Harriet Ziefert
M.A.T., New York University School of Education
Author, Language Arts Module,
Scholastic Early Childhood Program

PUFFIN BOOKS
Viking Penguin Inc., 40 West 23rd Street,
New York, New York 10010, U.S.A.
Penguin Books Ltd., Harmondsworth, Middlesex, England
Penguin Books Australia Ltd., Ringwood, Victoria, Australia
Penguin Books Canada Limited, 2801 John St., Markham, Ontario, Canada
Penguin Books (N.Z.) Ltd., 182–190 Wairau Rd., Auckland 10, New Zealand

First published in 1987
Published simultaneously in Canada
Text copyright © Harriet Ziefert, 1987
Illustrations copyright © David Prebenna, 1987
All rights reserved

ISBN 0-14-050745-0 Library of Congress Catalog Card No: 86-46222
Printed in Singapore for Harriet Ziefert, Inc.
HELLO READING is a trademark of Harriet Ziefert, Inc.

HELLO READING!™

A New House for Mole and Mouse

Harriet Ziefert
Pictures by David Prebenna

PUFFIN BOOKS

"This is a nice house," said Mole.
"I like it.
  Let's try everything out."

"Okay," said Mouse.
"We'll try everything out."

They tried the piano.

And the piano
worked just fine!

They tried the washtub.

The washtub worked just fine!

They tried the mixer.

And the mixer worked just fine!

They tried the bathtub.

And the bathtub worked just fine!

"I like this house," said Mole.
"Everything works just fine."

"Even the clock," said Mouse.
"Just listen to it tick-tock,
tick-tock, tick-tock, tock."

Then Mouse tried the bed.

Mole clicked the light ON...

and OFF!

And everything
worked just fine!

"I like this house," said Mole.
"Everything works just fine."

"But we haven't heard the doorbell ring," said Mouse.

"We have to wait for someone
to ring it," said Mole.
"Why?" asked Mouse.
"Because," said Mole.

So Mouse and Mole
waited and...
waited and...
waited.

"It's ringing," said Mole.
"Listen to the ding-dong,
 ding-dong, ding-dong, ding!"

Mouse opened the door.
"For you," said someone.
"The balloons are for you."

All of a sudden
everything was *not*
just fine!

"Help!" yelled Mouse.
"Help me!" he yelled.
"Help me, quick!"

Mole popped the balloons.
"Just listen," said Mole.
"Listen to the pip-pop,
    pip-pop, pip-pop, pop!"

Mouse landed on the piano.

Plunk!

And everything was just fine!